CW00840539

First published in 1996 by Sapling,
an imprint of Boxtree Ltd, Broadwall House,
21 Broadwall, London SE1 9PL
Copyright © Geoffrey Planer, 1996

10 9 8 7 6 5 4 3 2 1

Reproduction by SX Composing DTP
Printed and bound in Great Britain by Cambus Litho Ltd.

ISBN: 0 7522 2345 3

A CIP catalogue entry for this book
is available from the British Library.

MOUSE TALES

Mr Sinbad
Takes a Bath

Geoffrey Planer

sapling

For Granny Lesley and Papa
(definitely not Mr and Mrs Sinbad)

'Now, why so sad?' said Mrs Tail.
'Mr Bobbins is lost,' said Harry
as he washed his face.
'He'll turn up somewhere.'
'Won't.'
'I'm sure he will.'
'Not in time for bed,' said Harry.
'Well, cheer up anyway.'
'Can't.'
'Mr Sinbad did.'
'Did what?'
'Cheered up, for a minute or so.'
Mrs Tail sat down on the bed
and opened the book.

Another Night,
Another Mouse,
Another Tale . . .

Mr Sinbad
Takes a Bath

During the school holidays Mr St. John Sinbad was the most miserable person in town. His mouth was always turned down at the corners, he was always grumpy, he never said anything nice and he never smiled or laughed.

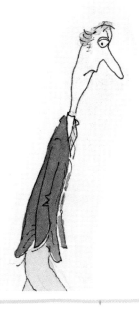

Mr Sinbad was a teacher at the school,
so that might have had something to do
with it. As the holidays drew to an end
and term time came closer and closer,
he became happier and happier.
Still miserable, of course, but a
happy sort of miserable.

In the long summer holiday, when Mr Sinbad was at his worst, his wife, Mrs Sinbad, would try to do nice things to cheer him up. She might put out his favourite supper, something like raw eggs and pencils with vinegar sauce.

Or she might sing opera to him in bed or
buy him a new book of extra long words
or tell him a joke in Latin –
that sort of thing.

Mr Sinbad would just thank her politely but he wouldn't smile

and he certainly never laughed.

One day in the middle of the long summer holiday, just as Mr Sinbad had come back home from a hard day of being bad-tempered to people in the street, Mrs Sinbad had a good idea.

She went upstairs to the bathroom and started to run a nice hot bath. She put some bubble bath in it,

put some soap in the dish,

laid out Mr Sinbad's towel

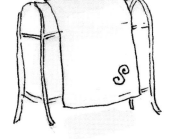

and his slippers and called him.

He got into the bath, grumbling away
as usual. Mrs Sinbad was standing
outside the bathroom. She was
a little disappointed.

'I know ...' she thought to herself.
'I'll really surprise him now.'

'Surprise, surprise! I'm coming in too!'
she shouted as she opened the door,
ran into the bathroom and jumped
into the bath with Mr Sinbad.

Mr Sinbad was indeed surprised.
He was so surprised that the
soap shot out of his hand.

It went up into the air.

And then it went down into his mouth,
which was unfortunately open in surprise.
He shut his mouth, but too late. The soap
slipped down his throat, down all the
little tubes, and into his tummy.

Mrs Sinbad didn't notice he had
swallowed the soap. Most people would
feel sick if they swallowed the soap, but
Mr St. John Sinbad was not like most
people and he felt funny. He felt tickly.

He jumped up in the bath and the soap
wiggled about in his tummy. It felt so
funny he started to laugh. He jumped
as he laughed and the soap slipped
around inside his tummy more.

It tickled and tickled.
He jumped and
wriggled and
held on to
his tummy,

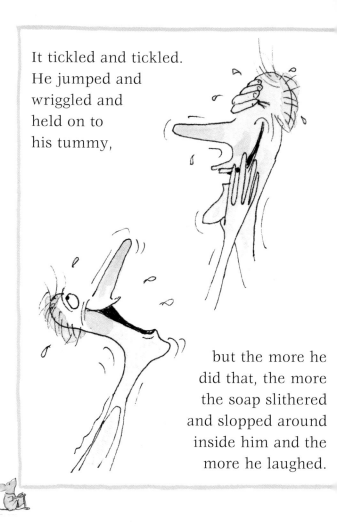

but the more he
did that, the more
the soap slithered
and slopped around
inside him and the
more he laughed.

And when he laughed, it jumped.
And when it jumped, it tickled.
And when it tickled, he laughed.
And he laughed and it tickled.

And it jumped and he laughed and
so on. He stood in the bath, soaking wet,
laughing and laughing. Mrs Sinbad
thought he was laughing at her.

She got quite cross ...

then crosser ...

then very cross.

She stood up and thumped
Mr Sinbad on the back.

Which was just the right thing to do, of course. The soap shot up the little tubes, out of his tummy and out of his mouth.

Everything stopped tickling.
He stopped laughing.
He started frowning again.

'Thank goodness he's back to normal,'
thought Mrs Sinbad, as they sat in
the bath scowling at each other.

'Look, I think I can see Mr Bobbins
under the bed,' said Mrs Tail.
'Shhh, he's asleep,' said Harry.
'But you said he was lost,' said Mrs Tail.
'I forgot, he went there to go to sleep,'
said Harry happily.
'Shall I get him out?'
'No silly. He's sleeping.'
'Oh,' said Mrs Tail. 'Silly old me.
Silly old Mr Bobbins bear.
Everything all right, then?'
'Yup,' said Harry happily as she tucked
his tail in and switched off the lamp.

Small Tales,
Tall Tales,
Bedtime -
for All Tails